Endpapers by Rebecca Wilson aged 10½.
Thank you to St Michael's C.E. Aided Primary School for helping with the endpapers – K.P.

To my lovely sister Moya and her beautiful husband Basil – V.T.
To Katya Wright – K.P.

## OXFORD
### UNIVERSITY PRESS

Great Clarendon Street, Oxford OX2 6DP

Oxford University Press is a department of the University of Oxford.
It furthers the University's objective of excellence in research, scholarship,
and education by publishing worldwide in

Oxford  New York

Auckland  Cape Town  Dar es Salaam  Hong Kong  Karachi
Kuala Lumpur  Madrid  Melbourne  Mexico City  Nairobi
New Delhi  Shanghai  Taipei  Toronto

With offices in

Argentina  Austria  Brazil  Chile  Czech Republic  France  Greece
Guatemala  Hungary  Italy  Japan Poland  Portugal  Singapore
South Korea  Switzerland  Thailand  Turkey  Ukraine  Vietnam

Oxford is a registered trade mark of Oxford University Press
in the UK and in certain other countries

First published 2003
First published in paperback 2004
Reissued with new cover 2006
2  4  6  8  10  9  7  5  3

British Library Cataloguing in Publication Data
Data available

ISBN-13: 978-0-19-272647-6 (paperback)
ISBN-10: 0-19-272647-1 (paperback)
ISBN-13: 978-0-19-272667-4 (paperback with audio CD)
ISBN-10: 0-19-272667-6 (paperback with audio CD)

Printed in Singapore

Valerie Thomas and Korky Paul

# Winnie's
## New Computer

OXFORD

UNIVERSITY PRESS

Winnie the Witch had a new computer. She was very excited. Her cat, Wilbur, was excited too. He thought something interesting might happen and he didn't want to miss it.

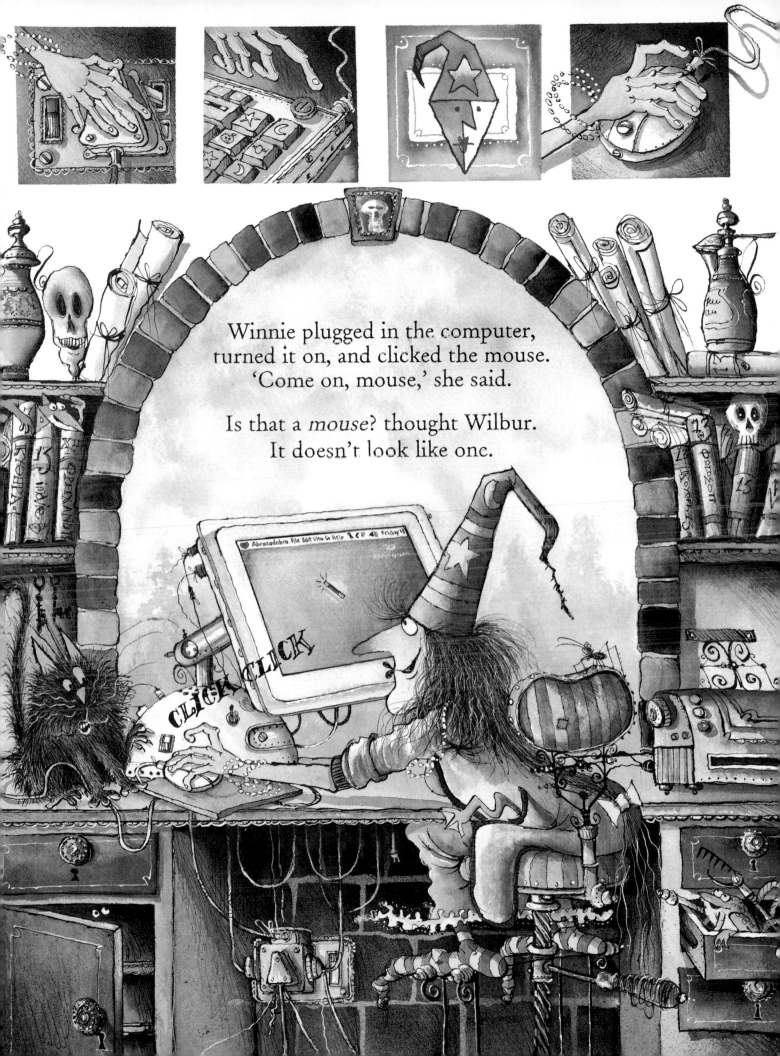

Winnie plugged in the computer,
turned it on, and clicked the mouse.
'Come on, mouse,' she said.

Is that a *mouse*? thought Wilbur.
It doesn't look like one.

Winnie went on to the internet.
Wilbur wanted a closer look at the mouse.
He patted it.

'Don't touch the mouse, Wilbur!' said Winnie.
'I want to order a new wand!'

Wilbur patted the mouse again. Pat, pat.

Winnie was cross.
She put Wilbur outside.
She didn't notice
that it was raining . . .

Wilbur noticed it was raining. He was getting wet.
He watched Winnie through the window.
She was having a good time.

She ordered her new wand, and then she
visited www.funnywitches.com.
They had some very funny jokes.
'Ha, ha, ha,' laughed Winnie.

Wilbur *wasn't* laughing.
The rain was dripping off his whiskers.
'Meeow,' he cried. ' Meeeoooww!'
But Winnie didn't hear him.

That mouse has put a spell on her, thought Wilbur.

CLICK CLICK

plop
Plop
plop
plop
plop
Plop
plop
plop
plop
plop
Plop

Plop, plop, plop.
'What's that noise?'
asked Winnie.

It was the rain.
It was coming through the roof.

'Oh no!' said Winnie. 'The rain
will ruin my new computer!
I need the Roof Repair Spell.'

But she couldn't find her book of spells
or her magic wand anywhere.

'Oh, where are they?' she cried
as the rain plopped down.

At last she found them.
She waved her wand seven
times at the roof, and shouted,

ABRACADABRA!

The roof stopped leaking.
'Thank goodness,' Winnie said.

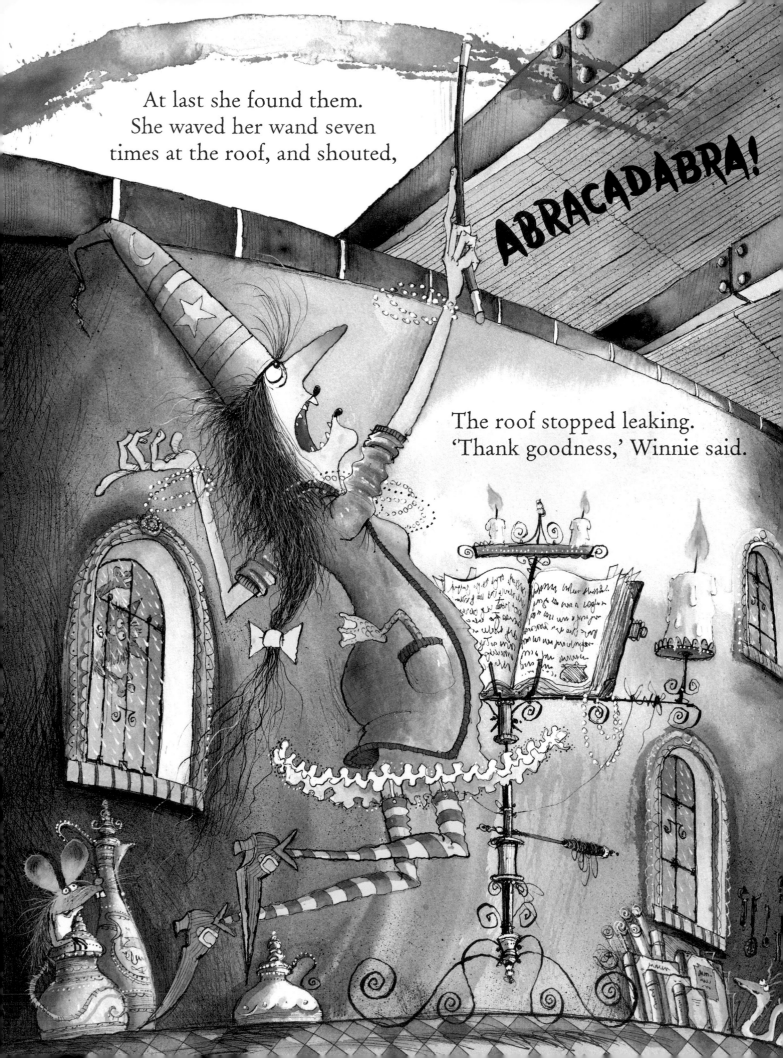

Then she had a wonderful idea.

'If I scan all my spells into the computer,' she said,
'I won't need my book of spells any more.
I won't need to wave my magic wand.
I'll just use the computer. One click will do the trick.'

So Winnie loaded all her spells into the new computer.
'I'd better try it out,' she said. 'What shall I do?'

'I know, I'll turn Wilbur into a blue cat.'

She let Wilbur inside. She went to
the computer, clicked the mouse,
and Wilbur was bright blue.

'Good!' said Winnie.
'It works!'

CLICK

CLICK

She clicked the mouse, and Wilbur was a black cat again.
An angry, wet, black cat.

'Well, Wilbur,' said Winnie, 'I won't need my book of spells or my magic wand any more.'

And she put them out for the dustman to take away.

That night, Wilbur waited until
he could hear Winnie snoring.
Then he crept downstairs.

He was going to see about that mouse.

He patted it.
Nothing happened.
'Meeow, grrrrsssss!' he snarled.
He grabbed the mouse, tossed it
into the air, and rolled onto his back.

Winnie had a lovely sleep.
In the morning she came downstairs
for her breakfast.

'Breakfast, Wilbur,' she called.
'Where are you, Wilbur?'

She looked in the garden, in the bathroom, in all the cupboards.
No Wilbur. Then she looked in the computer room . . .

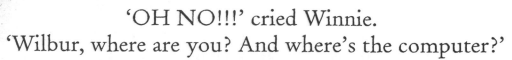

'OH NO!!!' cried Winnie.
'Wilbur, where are you? And where's the computer?'

She reached into the cupboard
for her book of spells. She put
her hand in her pocket for her
magic wand.

Then she remembered.

She ran to the window.
The dustman was tipping her
rubbish into his truck.

'Stop!' shouted Winnie. 'STOP!'
But it was too late. The dustman
couldn't hear her. He jumped
into his truck and drove away.

'What shall I do?' cried Winnie.

Then another truck came through the gate.
'My new wand!' said Winnie.
'It's arrived! Thank goodness!'

She grabbed the new wand, waved it once, and shouted,

**ABRACA**

The book of spells flew out of the rubbish truck, up into the air . . .

DABRA!

. . . and dropped into her arms.

Winnie rushed inside, and looked up the spell to make things come back.
Then she shut her eyes, waved her wand four times, and shouted,

# ABRACADABRA!

The computer and Wilbur came back.
'Oh, Wilbur!' said Winnie. 'You're bright blue!
Whatever happened?
Never mind, I'll change you back to black again.'

She went to the computer
and clicked the mouse.
Wilbur was a black cat again.

'Good,' said Winnie.
'It still works. But I think I'll keep my
book of spells and my magic wand.
I might need them one day.'